BURN THEM ALL

CONNOR WHITELEY

Any questions about the book, rights licensing, or to contact the author, please email connorwhiteley@connorwhiteley.net

DEDICATION

Thank you to all my readers without you I couldn't do what I love.

CHAPTER 1

Today was the day that the galaxy's fate was sealed and changed forever.

Ares Marsius, a genetically engineered superhuman soldier called an Angel of Death and Hope, stood in his massive bright silver lab with light pouring out of the walls, surgical instruments hanged and danced and swirled from the ceiling and everything was focused on a single metal slab that hovered ever so perfectly in the middle of the lab.

Ares had always loved his lab where he could ever so slightly mess with robots and humans and experiment with whatever he wanted, even though it was technically very illegal, but where was the fun in following all of the rules?

Ares stood there staring at the metal slab that added an almost supernatural depth of coldness and darkness to the lab, even though it was already icy and Ares was just glad that he was a superhuman so he could easily survive and thrive and deal with such temperatures.

But the little thing on the metal slab shivered slightly because Ares was trying to create a robot that looked and acted and behaved just like a real-life human. As his various instruments swirled and did their business from the ceiling, Ares enjoyed the smell of damp pine, flora perfume from his best friend Commander Georgia who had been here earlier, and the subtle hint of dried blood from an old test subject.

Ares liked the sound of the constant cutting, slicing and humming of the instruments as they continued to work, even Ares couldn't see what the final product or robot would look like, but he was excited to find out.

And just in case it looked like a monster, Ares was more than happy to chop it down with his two massive black battle-axes so no one would ever learn about his illegal creation.

All Ares had done was spend years perfecting the perfect method to his madness and he simply uploaded the designs into his computers and now he just hoped the computers could create something grand.

After all if he was going to rebel against the kind, generous and almighty Emperor of the Great Human Emperor, which considered Ares his favourite Legion Lord as he was in charge of an entire legion of Angels, he was going to need all the help he could possibly get.

Over the past year Ares and his best friend Georgia along with a few other of their closest generals in their rebellion that were the heads of other Legions, they had all been slowly moving their chess pieces into place so they could finally reveal themselves and rebel against the Emperor.

When Ares had reached out to the other legions, some of them didn't understand it in the slightest, not because they were opposed to the idea but because they couldn't understand why Ares of all people wanted to do it. Everyone knew he was going to rule the Empire when the Emperor died, he was the favourite and the Emperor would have done anything that Ares asked, but that really wasn't the point.

Ares had told everyone very plainly that the Emperor wasn't going to die, and Ares would never be in power so the Empire would improve, become fairer and he could never rule it with an iron-fist.

That was why Ares had invited everyone on board his newly repaired flagship, The Demigod, today so they could all make sure they were on the same page, and then Ares had to decide when they were going to reveal themselves and start the rebellion.

And hopefully kill the Emperor.

"Georgia is here to see you my Lord," a computerised voice said.

Ares flicked his wrist and a large round door at the far side of the lab opened and in came Commander Georgia, wearing a rather beautiful sterile white military uniform, white trousers and black boots but Ares only focused on the immense cannon had she had had attached to her arm when she lost it over a year ago, this one was definitely bigger and she had upgraded it for some reason.

"How goes the pet project?" Georgia asked.

Ares hated her calling it a *pet project*, if this worked then it could change the outcome of the war and she might become the Lord Commander of his Empire, and the most powerful woman in mankind's history.

Granted he sort of knew she had a point because he had been playing around with these human-robot things for thousands of years now since he was created 80,000 years ago, and they had always failed him, but Ares didn't exactly have much of a desire to lead his Legion for a few more hours and read battle reports or study languages like he normally loved.

"Anyway, came to tell you the first of the other Legion Lords have arrived, three more Battlegroups of Empire Army soldiers are here and the last of our forces would arrive within the next hour," Georgia said looking at the floor.

Ares laughed. "You wanting out?"

Georgia shot Ares a warning look, and Ares just knew that Georgia wanted this rebellion just as much as he did. Especially ever since they found an alien prophecy spelling out how Ares was meant to burn the galaxy to ash and then return as the Lord of War (which was his title within the Empire) and rule it angelically.

"It's just that this is actually happening now," Georgia said smiling. "We are about to plot the end of everything and how to kill the Emperor,"

Ares nodded as he focused on the instruments finishing up their work on the metal slab.

"But Ares," Georgia said carefully. "We must deal with our own forces first. There will be loyal elements within both mine and your forces, not including in the other Angel legions and Empire Army battlegroups,"

Ares nodded. That was definitely not a part of his plan that he was looking forward to, because as a Legion Lord the Angels that fell under his command were like children to him and best friends and brothers and sisters in arms, he never wanted to kill them, but if they were actually a threat to his rebellion then he was going to have to kill them.

And wipe out any of resistance that he encountered.

"We need to deal with them soon enough," Ares said. "Gather the other Legion Lords in the Empire Meeting Chamber and I'll be there as soon as I can," Ares said.

Moments later the air crackled, buzzed and hummed as the instruments unleashed energy into the air, smoke poured out of them and the instruments collapsed onto the floor.

Then the robotic monster of flesh and blood and brain matter that was made to be a perfect human-lookalike exploded into flames.

Ares quickly realised that if he made even a small mistake then him, his rebellion and even Georgia could end up exactly like that fleshy monster smouldering away in front of him.

He couldn't allow that to happen no matter how much it scared him.

CHAPTER 2

Commander Georgia of the Empire Army was actually rather surprised that Ares honestly believed she was stupid enough to wait in a chamber with a bunch of angry, horrible superhuman Legion Lords when he wasn't even in the room.

Instead Georgia had ordered her personal Angel escorts to get the Legion Lords into the meeting chamber but she was not going in there for a little while at least. Instead Georgia waited patiently in a little round security room with ugly grey walls, a few red holograms showing her some recent scans and other data that she wasn't that interested in at the moment.

Georgia had pushed the Angel-sized black chair to one side because she didn't want to sit down, she needed to be alert and focused and she needed to be ready in case things went badly.

As much as Georgia was tempted to switch on the security footage from the meeting chamber with the Legion lords, Georgia just wanted a few quiet moments to herself before all hell broke loose like it always did when some idiot was smart enough to put some many high ranking Angels in the exact same room.

So the little round security room was perfect for a few moments, but Georgia had to admit she was really looking forward to the rebellion finally getting underway. It might have smelt a little of sweat, peanuts and stale beer from the last baseline human officer to sit in here, but it was warm and enough for what Georgia wanted.

For now.

As a very high ranking member of the Empire Army, she had been seeking out Generals, Captains and Commanders to help her out in the rebellion, and thankfully she had recruited some of the most famous and deadly officials in the Great Human Empire.

Even if those officials were the first to die in the rebellion, their treachery would still be immense blows to the Empire, but Georgia still couldn't understand why everyone wanted to know what she got out of this little rebellion.

Georgia was still surprised that her fellow baseline humans had had the intelligence to understand that Ares was just in this for power, ambition and becoming Emperor, but they couldn't understand what she was after.

Even when her friends had questioned her on it, Georgia had laughed at them kindly because they couldn't seem to understand that unlike them, Georgia had grasped true power. A few years ago, Georgia had controlled and commanded and ruled over an entire of an entire Angel Legion and millions of her own forces against an enemy when Ares was busy fighting on a planet below.

Georgia had actually controlled superhumans and had them fight for her under her direct command. No other baseline human had ever had that power, had that ability to burn an entire solar system within hours if she desired, and she damn well wanted to always have that power.

And if she was Lord Commander of the Empire, then she would be in control of every single trooper, soldier and Angel in the entire Empire, and most humans could only barely understand the slightest of implications of what that meant.

But Georgia understood it all. She would be unstoppable.

An Angel knocked on the door behind her.

Georgia flicked her wrist and a seemingly invisible door in the little security room opened and two black armoured Angels, styled in the armour of medieval knights from ancient Earth, saluted her and stepped inside.

"Permission to speak frankly my Lord?" the tallest of the two male Angels said to Georgia's left.

Georgia nodded. She no longer felt afraid or scared or much of anything now whenever she was in the presence of these Demigods, because to Georgia they were just mortals now, and whatever magical powers normal humans believed Angels to have, those ideas have died long ago inside her.

"This is not right to have so many Legion Lords on the Demigod," he said. "I want to kill the Emperor just as badly as you do but this is not the way,"

Georgia subtly looked at the Angel on the right and he shook his head slightly. Georgia instantly knew that it was the shorter Angel's idea to bring the other to her, he probably doubted his friend's commitment to the rebellion and he was a threat.

Georgia was still amazed that Angels looked to her not as a human, but as a Superhuman commander and she really loved having that power and influence over them.

"This is what needs to happen. We need to formulate a plan against the Emperor and we cannot have this conversation over the communication networks in case a loyalist overhears them," Georgia said, tapping her cannon arm on the Angel-sized chair next to her.

The taller Angel didn't seem sure and Georgia could feel like he was weighting up his options.

"Spy," Georgia said coldly.

The taller Angel laughed. "Maybe I should be. The Emperor is right. The Emperor is-"

Georgia raised her cannon arm and fired.

A massive hole appeared in the taller Angel's chest before the corpse collapsed to the ground.

This was a lot worse than Georgia had ever thought possible, she had always been weary of trusting too many others with their rebellion plans before Ares officially revealed it to his own Legion and the wider Empire but clearly doubters were learning of it.

And it would only take one single doubter to tell the Emperor and loyal forces and then Georgia's plans and hopes and dreams might be dead long before the rebellion had ever begun.

"Thank you for bringing this to me," Georgia said. "What is your name?"

"Lokien," the black armoured Angel said.

Georgia nodded. She didn't know if she could trust him yet but given how he had been in contact with a danger to their rebellion, Georgia wanted him relatively close by for now just in case he was another danger to them.

"Walk with me Lokien," Georgia said as she left the little security room and started heading towards the Empire Meeting Chamber. "You're about to witness the fate of the Empire being decided,"

CHAPTER 3

Ares was absolutely sure that the Empire Meeting Chamber was the perfect place to conspire against the Emperor of the Empire considering this was a place that was designed for him to visit Ares. Ares had always liked its large oval shape and domed ceiling as diamonds, rubies and sapphires were embedded into the naturally bright white walls so they shone like stars guiding the Emperor towards his most favourite Legion Lord.

Ares really liked the bright blue oval meeting table in the very centre of the room with rich crispy meats, sweet juicy fruits and the most sensational vanilla ice cream spread out on it that Ares had ever tasted. Even now the sensational smell of it all made the taste of vanilla sundaes and dinner parties from his childhood form on his tongue.

Ares sat on a very comfortable grey metal chair at the head of the oval meeting table as he firmly placed his two massive battle-axes next to him as a show of strength against the other five Legion Lords that had cared to join him in his rebellion.

Out of the nine Angel legions that the Emperor created, Ares was more than glad that he had his legion and five others supporting him. And with each one specialising in an ability or certain way to attack the enemy, Ares was really looking forward to his quick victory.

Right next to Ares was thankfully Luna, legion Lord of the Sirens of The Emperor, a great Angel legion dedicated to Ares as Luna had indoctrinated her legion to believe that Ares was a god amongst them, so Ares doubted there would be any loyalists there to kill off.

Ares was also really glad to have the Legion Lords from the Raven Crow (infiltration specialists), Galaxy Burners (superhuman murderers and savages) and the Star Children (void warfare specialists) with him. As Ares focused on each of them he was starting to get more and more certain that he was going to win this rebellion.

But the only part of the Angel Legions that worried Ares was that male Legion Lord sitting just across from him at the very end of the oval meeting table, the Legion Lord of the Hydra legion, a strange and rather scary Angel legion that focused and specialised in disinformation and spying and Ares couldn't trust them as far as his superhuman arms could throw him.

"Thank you all for coming," Georgia said as she

came into the meeting chamber and stood directly behind Ares.

All the other Legion lords except Luna, because they had all met before, looked disgusted to have a baseline human in on the meeting but then Georgia tapped her cannon arm on the table, they were much quieter after that.

"What is the human doing here?" the Raven Crow Lord Macbeth said.

Ares focused on his harsh features that looked scarred, battle-hardened and he definitely wasn't an attractive man in the slightest, but in his oily black armour he did look powerful, and it was that power that Ares needed.

"I am Commander Georgia of the Empire Army and if you Angels want any hope of winning this rebellion then you need me and my forces,"

Everyone laughed.

"And what forces could the Empire Army have to face off against the might of the Angels?" the Legion Lord of the Galaxy Burners called Prometheus said.

Ares definitely wanted to be careful of that male Legion Lord. The Galaxy Burners were not a kind legion in the slightest and they were rude, reckless and Ares knew if anyone was going to destroy the rebellion, it would be that legion.

"I currently control twenty million troopers, one million destroyers and other ships," Georgia said. "If you really want to go against that as well as the three

Angel legions we all know we will not turn and the loyalists within the Empire Army. Then go ahead,"

Prometheus just sort of smiled and Ares just rolled his eyes because he had no doubt the Galaxy Burners would love to face off against every living thing in the galaxy.

"Everyone," Ares said. "We aren't here to fight yet. We are here to decide what will happen to the Empire. We need to decide how we are going to purge our own forces,"

All the Legion lords folded their arms and Ares knew the feeling. No matter the Legion, no legion Lord actually wanted to kill their own non-biological children and brothers and sisters in arms, but they were going to have to.

Georgia stepped forward. "We are going to have to kill them,"

Ares watched Prometheus look Georgia up and down as if he was examining how to kill her slowly and painfully, so Ares stood up.

"There are plenty of people still loyal to the Emperor within our ranks. Just because our six legions are mostly more loyal to us than the Emperor, doesn't mean everyone is," Ares said.

Everyone frowned even more.

"And if we don't kill off the loyalists," Ares said. "Then one of them will tell the Emperor what we are doing and things will get very bad for all of us,"

Ares was almost relieved to see that even the Hydra Legion Lord was nodding slowly and Ares had little doubt that the Hydra already knew exactly who in his legion needed to die.

And as much as Ares wanted to moan at the Hydra Legion for being so organised, it was exactly what all the legions needed to do at this moment in time.

But Ares had hardly expected it when the Hydra legion lord stood up and bowed at Ares. Ares hadn't expected one of the hardest-to-control legions to actually show him respect and the Hydra saluted Ares.

"You know me and my legion will always serve you, Lord Ares and Lord Georgia," he said. "And as a gesture of good fate I come with news saying that I have spies in the three loyalist legions and there is a noticeable chunk of anti-Empire forces in each one,"

Ares smiled. That was amazing news, even if the legions themselves didn't turn themselves over to his rebellion, then these large groups of anti-Empire Angels could become saboteurs and vital spies for him.

"Thank you," Ares said. "But we both know you're a very scheming person so I suppose you will control them in exchange for a seat as one of my top-Generals in the rebellion,"

"Well," the Hydra Legion lord said. "Now you mention it, of course,"

Ares and some of the others laughed, but Ares wasn't impressed. The Hydra Legion were cunning, scheming bastards that were evil to the core, and Ares wasn't exactly too pleased with the idea of having them so close to his rebellion that they could bring him and his plans crashing down.

Ares was about to talk more when Georgia tapped him on the shoulder and showed him a high security transmission from Earth, and Ares's second-on-command.

Empire forces from the loyal Ignis Legion had just arrived and they were demanding an audience with him alone on the authority of the Emperor himself.

Ares smiled to everyone like everything was in his complete control but he knew that was a complete and utter lie.

CHAPTER 4

Georgia really managed to surprise herself that her influence and dominating power over Angels extended a lot further than Ares' legion, because the moment the three Angel Captains from the Ignis legion saw her, they really, really wanted her in the room with them as they questioned Ares.

The very last thing that Georgia was opposed to was a spot of violent interrogation, but when the Ignis captains in their fiery red and orange Angel armour led her and Ares, who Georgia just knew was twitching to take out his massive battle-axes, inside a smaller oval meeting chamber with a flat ceiling, no chairs and dull grey walls, she wasn't that impressed.

Even the smell of the smaller meeting chamber was odd because it was stale, sweaty and clearly the enviro-systems hadn't been activated in this chamber for quite a while, but none of it explained why the Ignis Captains wanted to talk to Georgia and Ares.

"Why are you commanding six Angel legions?"

one of the captains asked.

Georgia forced herself not to smile as she continued to study and focus on the three captains. A few years ago she never could have told the difference between Angels in their armour but now she had been around them for so long, she was rather good at it now.

Georgia noticed that the Angel in the middle of the small group was a lot more demanding, confident and clearly the leader in this situation, which was great, because now she knew that the other two angels weren't captains in the slightest, they were only pretending to probably stop Georgia and Ares working out they were bodyguards.

So why did a loyal Legion feel the need to bring bodyguards onto Ares's flagship? Surely they were all friends here.

Georgia subtly made sure that her cannon arm was fully activated just in case she needed to quickly kill these enemy Angels, and needed to protect herself, Ares and the wider rebellion.

"We were meeting to discuss a key threat that the Hydra legion found," Ares said.

Georgia had to admit that was extremely clever of Ares, because if the Ignis Legion required proof of the intelligence, then it would seriously be child's play for the Hydra to create something and keep Earth happy. They had done it enough times before so Georgia couldn't see this time being any different.

"That is not what those on the Emperor's

Council believes," the real Angel Captain said.

Georgia was so looking forward to finally launching their rebellion and they would never have to deal with the stupidity of the Emperor's Council again. The group of twelve or Emperor knows how many leaders in the Empire that helped run it all, because they just seemed to be making one stupid decision after another.

And it was seriously starting to annoy Georgia a lot more than life itself.

"What did His Glorious Council say?" Ares asked as he winked at Georgia.

Georgia was just glad she was meant to be staying out of this conversation, it was far better to let the superhumans have their war of words and politics, and Georgia only step in if she needed to kill them.

"The Council proposes that you're staging a rebellion against the Emperor," the Ignis Captain said.

Georgia really had to force herself not to smile, because she was amazed how they had found out.

"Really?" Ares said like this was a joke. "Do you see any Anti-Empire posters or signs here? Do you actually think I would be stupid enough to do such a thing? Do you propose I have lost my mind?"

Even with the Ignis Angels wearing their helmets, Georgia absolutely knew they weren't smiling under them.

"The Ordo Infilitraticus sent a spy into this ship and the spy has since been murdered,"

Georgia felt her blood run cold as she realised that she hadn't been wrong to call that Angel a spy earlier. In fact that Angel probably wasn't one, it was probably a baseline human hacked and drugged up to look like an Angel.

Ares laughed softly. "You are being ridiculous. We have not killed an Angel, that is a crime and we are not traitors to the Emperor,"

All three Ignis Captains shook their heads.

"That is not for us to decide. We are under orders to bring you and the other six Legion Lords back to Earth for trial," the three Ignis said as one.

Georgia just looked at Ares for any sign about what to do. This simply couldn't be happening, the Empire was on to them but clearly didn't have any prove or otherwise they would be under attack and the Ignis would be killing them instead of escorting them back to Earth.

Ares simply nodded at the Ignis. "Of course,"

Georgia was completely amazed that Ares was actually going to put up with this rubbish, they had a rebellion to plan and reveal and deal with. They didn't have time to play around with loyalist Angels and trials.

"Just give me one hour," Ares said. "To gather up my forces and get them to ready to departure,"

"Actually," Georgia said. "Due to the immense size of our forces we will need two hours to get all the warships and cruisers and destroyers ready for departure back to Earth,"

Georgia felt the Ignis stare at her like they were trying to burrow into her very soul as they just stood there in silent before they nodded.

"Two hours then we are heading back to Earth and any signs of you trying to deceive us, get rid of us or kill us and you will be declared as traitors," the Ignis Captain said.

Georgia and Ares simply nodded and bowed.

As Georgia led Ares out of the meeting chamber and down a very long bright white corridor, he simply smiled at her and oddly enough she actually smiled too.

Not because they weren't in deep shit and their plans and rebellion were hanging by a knife's edge but because they only had two hours to save it all.

Otherwise they were all going to die.

And the next two hours were going to be extremely fun indeed.

CHAPTER 5

Over the past two hours, or one hour and fifty minutes to be precise, Ares had honestly heard some of the bravest, stupidest and weirdest ideas he had ever heard, and over the past ten of thousands of years he had been alive, he had definitely heard a lot of them.

Ares had loved how Georgia had suggested they simply unleash their rebellion now and kill the Ignis escorts, but Ares just knew that wouldn't have worked, so he suggested going back to Earth for the trial. But then Georgia had suggested something that Ares could only describe as absolute beautiful genius.

They were going to trick the Empire into forgetting about the possible rebellion.

The delicious scents of juicy roasted pork, crispy fried chicken and sweet bread that would melt into buttery deliciousness filled the air as Ares held his two massive battle-axes inside a very small oval chamber with grey walls, a single bright orb of light overhead and Georgia was patiently standing next to him.

And the Legion Lord of the Hydra legion was facing them, arms crossed and he did look imposing in his blood red battle armour that he had changed into.

Ares had called him because if Georgia's plan was going to work at all, then he was going to need the Hydra Legion to quickly create some false information about a massive threat that would cause the Treason Trial to be put on the back burner whilst the Empire focused on the bigger threat.

Ares just didn't know if the Hydra would be interested in such a great idea, or what Ares was a lot more concerned about was what it would actually cost him to get the Hydra to agree to such a bargain.

The sound of the ship hummed, vibrated and popped as Ares just knew that the Ignis escorts were docking in the hangar and they were preparing to make sure that all ships and legions suspected of treachery were under strict Empire control.

The Hydra just laughed, and for a Legion Lord Ares was rather impressed he was so carefree given the situation.

"What do you need?" the Hydra asked looking at Ares.

Ares looked at Georgia and she was subtly tapping her cannon arm in her fleshy hand.

"I'll make you one of my top generals if you create a package of disinformation making the Empire forget about us," Ares said.

The Hydra smiled. "What sort of information would you like me to spread?"

Georgia stepped forward. "Let's cut to the chase. You might think you have an option to play difficult here but when the Ignis legion find out you are still aboard the Demigod in less than ten minutes your legion will be declared a traitor. Do you really want your Angels to die?"

Ares really smiled at Georgia, because that was exactly how he would have put it in a few precious moments. Especially as the Ignis legion had ordered all Legion Lords, under the Emperor's authority, to return to their flagships and not to mix or even communicate with anyone else.

The punishment was death.

The Hydra bowed his head a little. "I'll admit this *human* has fight in her but she is right. I will wage a war later on about what position I want for myself and my legion but right now disinformation must rule,"

The Hydra looked like he was about to continue when he just stopped and it almost looked like he was in pain.

In fact this was probably the first time ever that Ares had actually seen the Hydra bending to the will of another. Normally the Hydra legion were literally laws upon themselves and that alone caused tons of conflict with the Empire Army, other Angel legions and even the secret policing organisation of the Inquisition.

"I'll do whatever you need," the Hydra said. "What do you need me to do exactly?"

Ares smiled at Georgia, finally something was going their way and Ares just hoped that their good luck would continue for a little bit longer.

The entire Demigod hummed a little longer as Ares realised that the Ignis legion were attaching a destroyer or some other warship of theirs to the actual hulk.

This was getting way too serious for Ares's liking.

"Create a battle report or intelligence report about some kind of extremely dangerous alien threat that is amassing on the edges of Empire space," Ares said.

The Hydra shook his head. "It would have to be so carefully done. It couldn't come from any of our six traitor legions, the alien threat would have to seem real enough, and what about the damage?"

Ares wasn't sure what he meant.

"What if," the Hydra asked, "we create a fake report, the Empire sends spies to the region and they discover no damage or evidence of the threat?"

Ares shrugged. He had a serious feeling that his luck had just run out and considering there was less than a minute until the Ignis deadline Ares seriously knew that this option was most probably a dead end.

"What about en-route back to Earth?" Georgia asked.

"What?" Ares asked.

"They're going to escort us back right?" Georgia

asked.

Ares nodded.

"So what if there is a threat discovered en-route back to Earth, we past it and the Ignis legion receive a report that makes them stop escorting us and wants to investigate the fake threat?" Georgia asked.

Ares wasn't sure about this in the slightest, he much preferred the idea of creating a fake intelligence report about a threat so far away that it was only possible for Ares and his traitor forces to deal with it, forcing the Ignis legion not to escort them back to earth but help them investigate the fake threat.

But Georgia's idea might be better but it was a lot less controlled. All the routes back to Earth were heavily defended, scanned and security was extreme.

It would be impossible to attack or run away from the Ignis Legion without revealing the rebellion before they were ready.

Ares just didn't see another option.

"Do it," Ares said.

Georgia nodded and the Hydra just smiled as he contacted his forces and Ares really hoped that this plan wouldn't get them all killed.

CHAPTER 6

Georgia had absolutely no faith whatsoever about her plan or deception against the Ignis legion, and now sadly only time would tell and Georgia just seriously hoped it would work as she stood on the massive oval bridge of the Demigod.

Georgia had always loved its massive floor-to-ceiling windows that allowed her to stare at the cold deadly void of space as it all rushed past her, and the three tiers of command crew hunched over holographic computers that lined the edges of the oval bridge.

Thankfully, the command crew's beautiful aromas of bitter coffee, creamy Danish rolls and other glorious sticky pastries were on full force today, so the entire bridge stunk of the amazing aromas and Georgia just loved it when that happened. She knew that Ares wouldn't like it in the slightest because of his superhuman senses but she had much bigger problems right now.

The Angel Georgia had found earlier called Lokien stood right next to her still emotionless wearing his Angel helmet, and Georgia had already checked three times that her cannon arm was fully activated just in case she needed to kill him.

Georgia wasn't completely sure if he was a spy or not considering he had bought another spy to her. A lot of her Empire Army friends would have said that him turning in another spy would prove his innocence, but they were always stupid like that.

And Georgia couldn't afford such a silly risk.

The shocking silence of the bridge made Georgia's stomach uneasy and she kept checking over her shoulders every few minutes at the ten Angels in the Ignis Legion's fiery red armour lining the edges of the bridge, just in front of the tiers of command crew.

It wouldn't have mattered even if the Ignis guards didn't have their fingers tightly round the triggers of their superhuman guns, Georgia would have felt just as uneasy.

And it wasn't like the fact that Ares had decided to spend a little more "illegal" time with the Hydra was making her feel better, because right at this moment she was in charge of the entire rebellion with Ares busy and if she made a single mistake in front of these Ignis guards they were all as good as dead.

"Commander," a booming female said.

Georgia slowly turned around and bowed slightly to a very tall female Angel in fiery red armour of the Ignis Legion and the large medal over her right breast denoted her as a Commander herself, but commanders and Angels never tended to wear their medals on official business so Georgia was a little unsure of why this Angel wanted Georgia to know her rank.

"Thank you for bowing my friend," the Angel said. "I am Commander Sadle of the 2nd Ignis Company,"

Georgia was a little surprised that such a high ranking member of the Ignis Legion would come on this mission. Whilst Georgia wasn't 100% sure of how the Angel companies worked in terms of military structure, she was fairly sure that Commanders were the highest ranking and leaders of the company.

So why bring someone so important onto a mere escort mission?

"It is an honour my friend," Georgia said. "I have heard much about the 2nd company and I am sure after this misunderstanding has been cleared up that you and me can learn from each other,"

It was a complete and utter lie that Georgia had heard anything about the 2nd company, but she liked lying to superhumans and it was a long trip back to Earth so Georgia just needed a little entertainment.

"You think this is a misunderstanding?" Sadle asked.

"Of course," Georgia said like the alternative was impossible. "I have served with Lord Ares for a long time, he is loyal to the Glorious Emperor and I will personally kill him if he is a traitor,"

Sadle smiled a little. "For some reason I do not doubt that my dear,"

Georgia watched Lokien out of the corner of her eye, he might have been wearing his helmet but Georgia could just feel that he was smiling at her, willing her to make a mistake, or maybe this whole damn rebellion was simply making her paranoid.

Hell, the entire command crew still didn't even know about the rebellion, but they were the least of Georgia's concerns, they were all so amazing that Georgia doubted there were any loyalists amongst them.

"We will reach Earth in three months and then the trial will begin and the Angels will be found guilty," Sadle said.

Georgia simply nodded, because Sadle made an excellent point about all of this trial business, the Ignis escorts had probably been travelling to their location for three months, so they had to know about the rebellion or been suspicious of it for three months, or because of how the Empire's wheels of bureaucracy worked maybe even a year ago.

So how did the Empire find out?

Georgia just looked at Lokien and realised that Georgia really couldn't trust anyone but Ares. It was so possible that the other Legion Lords had spies in their legions that told the Empire, or hell, maybe a Legion Lord betrayed Georgia and Ares.

Literally anything was possible at this point.

A red flashing light appeared on the massive

floor-to-ceiling windows, and Georgia gestured to Sadle that she was going to answer it. Sadle nodded which Georgia took as an agreement.

Georgia flicked her wrists and a long line of red holograms showed up detailing out intelligence reports, numbers of ships destroyed and a mysterious enemy moving about a nearby sector killing everything they touched.

Georgia was flat out amazed at how realistic and detailed the fake information looked then she heard the bridge's doors open.

"What is it?" Ares asked.

Georgia smiled because this had to be part of the act but when she turned around and showed Ares' the information his face hardened.

"This wasn't us," Ares said quietly.

Georgia just nodded like Ares had given her a critical order.

Georgia couldn't believe what was happening because if they didn't create a massive threat that made the Empire want them to deal with it instead of going on trial. Then what the hell was the threat?

And why was the threat more important than the possibility of superhuman traitors?

CHAPTER 7

Ares flat out couldn't believe what a mistake this all was and how badly it was all getting out of control, as he stood on the massive oval bridge of the Demigod with its grey walls, massive floor-to-ceiling windows and tiers of command crew and holographic computers. This was not going well.

The disgusting, outrageous smell of bitter coffee, damn Danish rolls and other pastries filled the air and that just pissed Ares off even more than this damn information. All the bloody Hydra had to do was create some fake information but instead real intelligence was coming in thick and fast and Ares just hated being out of control like this.

And Ares was seriously not impressed with the ten stupid Ignis Angels lining the oval bridge and there was a new commander that Ares hadn't seen before standing right next to Georgia. All Ares wanted to do to that commander was rip into her flesh with his two battle-axes, but sadly that wasn't an option.

For now.

"Commander Sadle," the new Angel Commander said bowing slightly. Ares gave the female Angel a little nod of respect even though her and her forces didn't deserve it in the slightest.

Ares subtly looked at Georgia's smooth beautiful face and she just looked excited more than anything else, and that was exactly why Ares loved her like a sister.

"Command crew," Ares said. "Pull up the incoming information in holographic form,"

The command crew quietly muttered to themselves as an immense red hologram appeared of a nearby solar system with a dying star and only five planets.

Ares recognised it as a solar system about four hours from their current location, it was actually the location that the Hydra was going to send them too, but there was something different about the solar system now compared to when him and the Hydra looked at it.

It had three planets less.

"Bring up historical Empire records on the system," Ares said.

Georgia took a few steps forward and Ares was really glad to have her at his side, if this was a massive problem then both of them needed to decide if this was a threat or an opportunity for their rebellion. They were a team after all.

"Don't bother," Sadle said, and the entire bridge just looked at Ares.

Ares was rather amazed that a mere Commander had the balls to dismiss a command from a legion lord.

"Excuse me?" Ares asked.

"I was stationed in the system two hundred years ago and three planets were missing," Sadle said.

At least he had it confirmed now, but Ares still really didn't like the woman.

Ares flicked his wrist a little and massive leaf-like spaceships appeared in holographic form around the planets, then details of Empire ships, planets and space stations destroyed filled with the holograph.

Ares had studied a lot of alien races in the galaxy and their languages and cultures but he had never seen an alien race using leaves before, at least as part of their ship designs.

The holographic display was far too grainy for Ares to make out what sort of leaves the ships looked like, but he was interested to say the least. Because how did an alien race infiltrate an Empire system surrounded by rather heavily fortified systems?

"Bring up directional data of the enemy," Georgia said, clearly having the same idea.

The hologram zoomed out and revealed the aliens had travelled in from two directions, both over the galactic plane and below it.

"Shit," Georgia said.

Ares had rarely heard Georgia swear in all the

years he had served with her and been friends too, so whatever she had apparently worked out, it had to be bad.

"Zoom out more and plot trajectory," Georgia said.

Ares had no clue where she was going with this because it was crystal clear that the aliens had to come from outside the Milky-way Galaxy, otherwise they wouldn't have needed to come under and over the galactic plane.

As the hologram zoomed out even more and a blue dotted line plotted the course of the aliens, Ares's superhuman stomachs twisted as he realised that Georgia was right. The aliens hadn't come from outside the galaxy, they had come very much from inside.

By the time the hologram had revealed the starting location of the aliens with leave-shaped spaceships, Ares was amazed that they had come from the very edges of Empire territory.

But Ares just couldn't understand why the aliens would travel above and below the galactic plane instead of traveling straight through it like humans did?

Ares heard the clicking and aiming of superhuman guns.

Georgia reflexed up her cannon arm.

Ares forced himself not to whip out his battle-axes as he saw that Sadle and her ten Angels had their weapons firmly fixed on Ares.

"Lord Ares," Sadle said, "under the authority given to me by the Emperor, you cannot go to this location. You are set to travel to Earth to be found guilty of treason,"

Ares really wanted to kill this woman right now, because she was seriously being a pain in the ass.

"This is a threat to the Empire," Ares said. "I am loyal to the Emperor. I want to investigate this information and find out what happened to our forces. Surely the safety of the Empire is more important than some trial that will find me innocent?"

Ares loved watching Sadle react, work out and study his features as she too tried to figure out if the other was going to buckle.

Ares certainly wasn't.

"I will contact Earth and Lord Ignis himself," Sadle said, "then it will be up to them to decide what your fate will be,"

Ares gave her a mocking bow as she left and the ten Angels relaxed ever so slightly but Ares just knew that those Ignis Angels would fire given the smallest of excuses.

Ares carefully gestured Georgia to come closer to him and she did.

"Now our fates are firmly in the hand of the Hydra. I just hope that he sees this situation and makes it sound so bad to Earth that they have to let us investigate," Ares said.

Georgia gave him a weak smile.

He couldn't agree more. Out of all the traitor

legion lords Ares wanted to determine his fate. The Hydra was at the very bottom of that list.

Ares just hoped he wasn't going to regret this.

CHAPTER 8

Georgia seriously wanted nothing more than to just kill this stupid Sadle woman as Georgia stared out of the massive floor-to-ceiling windows on the oval bridge of the Demigod, but apparently Ares believed that would be far too counterproductive to their rebellion. At this point Georgia seriously couldn't have cared less, Sadle was just an idiot pawn of the Emperor that needed to die a very slow and painful death.

But as that was impossible for the moment, as Georgia never wanted to upset her brother-from-another-mother, Georgia just rested her cannon arm in her fleshy hand and just waited for the amazing chance to use it.

"I understand Lord Ignis," Sadle said.

Georgia forced herself not to smile and out of the corner of her eye, she could see that Ares was struggling to do the same as he was standing next to her left, then Lokien (someone she was definitely growing more and more distrustful of) stood to her right.

"May the Flame Protect You," Sadle said.

Georgia hated that stupid part of Ignis Legion culture, and Georgia realised that the Empire really was a bag of stupid contradictions, because religion was illegal because it was a cancer on humanity, but then the Empire allowed the Sirens of the Emperor to exist and the Ignis legion to have their mythology about a flame being from their homeworld.

It was pathetic.

A few moments later Sadle marched over to Georgia, and her and Ares just smiled at Sadle as the tall woman in fiery red armour simply frowned at both of them.

"I do not agree with my Legion Lord or Earth but you two have your wish," Sadle said.

Georgia gave Sadle a mocking bow and she was so tempted right at that moment to confirm the rebellion was true, especially with Sadle not being able to do anything because she now had more important orders, but Georgia forced herself to behave and that was not something that came naturally to her in such situations.

"Open a fleet wide channel," Ares said to the command crew.

Georgia turned her back to Sadle and followed Ares into the centre of the oval bridge and she hissed as the icy coldness of the rough marble floor sent chills through her military boots.

"Done," a command crew member said.,

"This is Lord Ares," he said, "we now have new orders to travel to the…"

"Noir System," Georgia said, telling Ares the name of their target.

Ares told his forces the name of the system. "Our orders are to investigate the alien threat and stop it before it costs more Empire lives,"

As Ares cut the transmission, Georgia folded her arms (which was difficult enough when one of her arms was a cannon) and she was rather interested in learning more about the enemy from the information they had received, but Georgia really wanted to know where the information came from.

"Where did the information come from?" Georgia asked.

Ares got out his two massive battle-axes and the ten Ignis guards on the bridge tensed a little.

"Command crew?" Georgia asked.

"The system itself. They sent all the information as a distress beacon," a woman said.

Georgia shook her head. That couldn't be right in the slightest because there were hundreds of thousands of Empire worlds, ships and battle groups between the Demigod and its massive fleet and the Noir System.

So why did Georgia and Ares only get the information?

"Are we sure we're the only people to get the intelligence?" Georgia asked.

Ares cursed under his breath as the command crew nodded, Georgia was seriously getting concerned.

Sadle stepped forward. "Are you two traitors trying to tell me that as the Noir system was burning, under attack and everything else, the very last act of defiance couldn't have been trying to get help and that is some kind of trick?"

Georgia nodded. "You might be an Angel Commander but you are blind. If your Legion and homeworld was burning, would you really make sure you only transmitted your information to a fleet so far away that you would need a lot of time to setup the transmission?"

Georgia loved how Sadle's face dropped, because that was the truth. Georgia was really starting to doubt if the Noir system had ever been under-attack like the intelligence, not from the Hydra legion, implied.

"If that's true," Sadle asked. "Then who the hell could have created this intelligence that was good enough to foul the Hydra?"

Georgia just looked at Ares for a moment, she had no clue what Sadle was talking about, as far as she knew the Hydra hadn't looked at the information, in fact none of the Legion Lords had minus Ares.

"You spoke with the Hydra?" Ares asked.

Georgia was only noticing the microscopic note of fear in his voice and Georgia quickly realised that the Hydra was still probably on board against Sadle's wishes.

"I did," Sadle said. "And my forces did locate the point on this ship that he was located and he has been arrested and is on a separate warship back to Earth to stand trial immediately,"

"Damn it," Georgia said quietly and by accident.

This was not what they needed in the slightest, now the Hydra Legion was basically out of action and they were a powerful ally to have in the rebellion, Georgia just had no clue if they were still allies or if with the Hydra being arrested if that had taken their help completely off the table.

"What will happen to their Angels?" Georgia asked.

Sadle smiled as she focused on the coldness of space and stars and nearby planets through the massive floor-to-ceiling windows.

"They are all being arrested and put to sleep as we speak. They will all be entering a state of sleep until they reach Earth and their fate is decided per standard protocol,"

Georgia nodded like that was a great idea. But if the Ignis legion, and by extension the wider Empire, were so calm and uncaring towards damning an entire Legion of Angels that were numbered into the millions then no one was safe.

Georgia, Ares and the rest of their allies were not safe in the slightest and that scared Georgia a damn slight more than she ever wanted to admit.

CHAPTER 9

Over the next four hours, Ares just focused on the outrageous and disgusting smells of bitter coffee, damn Danish rolls and other so-called pastry delights that the command crew simply kept ordering from the food synthesisers, and as much as Ares really, really hated the smell as he stood studying streams upon streams of data on the oval bridge of the Demigod, it was exactly what he needed.

After the four hours of travel time to the Noir system, Ares was completely stumped about what alien they could be facing. He normally prided himself on knowing everything about aliens, their cultures and their languages and their spaceships, but Ares had never ever seen any alien race act like this or use leaf-shaped spaceships.

And it was even worse that there wasn't a single spelling or grammatical mistake in the information and intelligence the aliens presumably sent Ares, so they had to be extremely smart.

Smart aliens always worried Ares.

"Entering system now," a man said from the command crew.

Ares tore his eyes away from the streams upon streams of data and looked out on the small Noir system through the massive floor-to-ceiling windows.

Ares ran his fingers gently over the cold metal of his two massive battle-axes for comfort more than anything else as Georgia stood firmly next to him, and her "friend" Lokien stood next to her.

The Noir System was rather dark even accounting for the sad fact that their star was dying, and Ares had checked the historical records and the Noir system used to be extremely bright but now it only seemed to be weakly pulsing light.

It was just enough light to make the five remaining planets barely visible with their long-dead jungles, black abysses of oceans and any life that existed on these worlds were now long gone.

But Ares couldn't see a single chunk of wreckage, annihilated space station or even a leaf-shaped spaceship. There was nothing here. Ares couldn't even see the shattered remains of three planets like he had believed there to be.

"Scan the system," Ares said.

The command crew typed, swiped and tapped away at their holographic computers as Ares stepped closer to his beautiful sister-like Georgia.

"Something is very wrong here," he said.

Georgia smiled. "No shit,"

Ares playfully hit her. "Seriously. We've lost the Hydra Legion, I have little doubt the other legions aren't far behind, we're in a system with an unknown enemy-"

Ares was going to continue when Georgia waved him silent, something he was still getting used to. As the Emperor's favourite, Ares was used to answering only to the Emperor himself, but somehow Georgia could just hold him to account like she was the real leader of the rebellion.

And sometimes it definitely felt like it.

"Stop thinking of these aliens as the enemy," Georgia said. "The Anti-alien mentality is why the Empire is a rotting corpse, you and me have learnt a lot from aliens, haven't we?"

Ares rolled his eyes and smiled. That was why he loved her like a sister, because she was rarely wrong. Ares had learnt about the prophecy that planted the seeds of his rebellion from aliens, he had learnt about the brainwashing mindcamps from aliens that were bound to be critical in the war ahead so Ares couldn't see why aliens couldn't teach him something this time.

"My lord," an Ignis Angel said.

Ares and Georgia focused on Sadle as she went over to her Angels and they started talking.

As much as Ares loved his superhuman hearing this time it was just useless.

"Here," a female member of the command crew said.

A large red hologram formed in the middle of the oval bridge and highlighted a single leaf-shaped ship that was messing with their scanners. There was no other ship, fighter or anything around it.

But Ares was more focused on its size, even from the poor scale of the hologram, Ares could tell that it was massive. Maybe the size of a moon or a dwarf planet, but it still made no sense as to why bring a ship that big into this system.

"Can we contact it?" Georgia asked.

Lokien laughed next to her. "Of course not my Lord,"

Ares and Georgia both glared at Lokien.

"Why not?" Ares asked.

"Because of our guests. Talking to aliens is a crime," Lokien said.

The sad thing was that Lokien wasn't wrong, and that just annoyed Ares, he hated lesser Angels that he didn't even know being right instead of him.

"Stop," Sadle said as her and her ten Ignis Angels walked over to them.

Ares just rolled his eyes. All he wanted to do was get started with the mission and the rebellion and the damn Ignis legion just kept interfering with his plans.

"What?" Georgia asked struggling to fold her arms.

"My Angels have confirmed to me that my peers stationed on the flagships of the Star Children, Galaxy Burners and Raven Crow Legions have been attacked," Sadle said.

Ares felt his stomachs twist into a painful knot. This was not good in the slightest, Ares had commanded those idiots not to attack.

"My forces managed to take control of the flagships, subdue the Legion Lords and now what happened to the Hydra Legion will happen to those three legions as well," Sadle said coldly.

Damn it. This entire plan was falling apart, this wasn't going well at all, and it was only a matter of time until Ares was attacked or had to defend himself against the Ignis legion.

Ares was really amazed that Georgia was still smiling at Sadle like Georgia was still fully in control of the situation, Ares really wished he felt like that.

Ares was losing allies and powerful troops by the hour. He needed a new plan.

"My lord Ares!" a woman shouted from the command crew.

"The leaf ship," someone else said. "It's powering up. It's moving towards us,"

"Battle stations," Sadle said.

Ares just glared at her. He was the commander of his fleet not her.

"The leaf ship is trying to contact us," someone else said.

Ares and Georgia looked at each other and smiled this was exactly what they had been waiting for.

Ares just looked at Sadle. "May we answer it,"

Sadle didn't look sure.

"Leaf ship's weapons are charging," someone said.

Ares prepared himself to whip out his battle-axes to kill Sadle if she refused.

"Answer it damn it," Sadle said.

Ares really smiled because it proved a point. Sadle was nothing more than a scared little Angel.

And scared people were much easier to kill when the time came but Ares had to deal with the leaf ship first before anything else.

And that really excited him.

CHAPTER 10

Georgia absolutely loved having the amazing chance to actually talk to the brilliant, if not slightly scary, aliens that had lured them here on purpose, most probably for some kind of evil purpose but if there was even a sliver of a chance that they were allies against the Empire than Georgia was seriously going to take the risk of talking to them.

Inside the massive oval bridge of the Demigod, Ares flicked his wrists and Georgia stood firmly next to him with her cannon arm at the ready in case the communication was dangerous or anything. And even the ten Ignis guards and stupid Sadle had their superhuman guns firmly at the ready just in case.

Moments later a very large light blue hologram appeared of a humanoid creature that looked to be blurred so Georgia couldn't make out any details perfectly.

"I am-"

"I know who you are Ares of the Empire

superhumans Angels of Death and Hope," the hologram said.

Georgia wasn't impressed with the velvety smoothness of the voice. It was almost so human that Georgia was starting to doubt if they were dealing with aliens at all.

And the hologram bothered Georgia too, it was weird for an alien race to have such great technology that they could build ships the size of moons but not have good technology to clearly project a hologram of themselves.

It made no sense.

A bright blinding golden light shot out of the projector.

Georgia felt ice cover her skin. She froze.

Moments later the ice shattered around her but Georgia was surprised that the entire bridge was covered in a thick layer of ice.

All the command crew, the bridge and the Ignis Angels were completely covered in crystal clear ice that kept them completely frozen and unable to move.

"Thank you for freeing her," Ares said.

Georgia looked around to see that Ares, herself and another figure were the only living things not covered in ice.

Georgia focused on the other figure in the bridge and she was pleased to see something so beautiful, elegant and almost divine.

The figure was definitely humanoid-shaped with

its long slim legs and arms made from little shards of crystal that light beamed out from. The figure's chest was dangerously thin and made up from thousands of little crystal shards that pulsed light probably in time to its heartbeat and its head was nothing more than a twisted mimic of a damaged human face made from diamonds.

The figure might have been beautiful but it looked dangerous, strange and unnatural, and Georgia didn't still understand what was happening with people being frozen in ice.

"Relax Star Child," the figure said, its voice smooth and seductive. "I needed Ares to be alone but he insisted on having you next to him,"

Georgia nodded her thanks to Ares.

"We have been following you for a long time Lord of War," the figure said. "You have done some impressive things and this is where the timestreams needed our paths to converge,"

As much as Georgia wanted to call out this alien or whatever he was for lying or being some kind of mythic, Georgia just knew he was telling some kind of truth and that they did actually need him.

"The timestreams?" Ares asked. "You make it sound like we're each other's destiny or something,"

The figure's laughter was soft and angelic, not what Georgia was used to at all.

"I do not quite know about that Lord Ares but I do know we are meant to meet at this moment and help each other,"

Georgia shook her head. "That means you want something and in my experience people who burn solar systems and destroy planets never want something manageable,"

The figure tipped her head forward. "I understand the human's concern but it is not well-founded. I burned this solar system, correct. I took all the human debris, corpses and annihilated planets into my ship, correct. But I want to help you in exchange for something small,"

Georgia frowned at Ares and the fact that he was actually considering listening to this alien fool spoke volumes. Georgia didn't trust this alien any more than she trusted Lokien at this point.

"What do you want?" Ares asked.

The figure smiled and bowed and took a step forward.

"I want to live inside your battle-axes,"

Georgia laughed. That was the weirdest request she had ever heard and she had heard some crazy ones in her military service.

Ares folded his arms. "What are you?"

"I am the last of my species, the Dawned Ones, a shape-shifting alien race that witnessed the Big Bang and have documented the galaxy since the first living thing developed,"

Georgia wasn't buying it.

"My species once worked in the shadows and guided the species of the galaxy towards peace, wealth and democracy but we made a lot of enemies. They started attacking us and in the end even our friends turned against us that was millions of years go,"

Georgia was glad that judging by Ares's frown, he wasn't buying it either.

"And you survived?" Ares asked. "And now you want to come out of hiding for the sake of what? Helping us destroy the Empire,"

The Figure looked shocked and panicked.

"What!" the figure shouted. "You want to destroy the Empire! No. You cannot. I thought you were friendly,"

Georgia whipped out her cannon aiming it at the figure.

Ares whipped out his battle axes.

"No," the figure said. "The timestreams lied. They told me to be friends with you. They told me to help you save the Empire. They told me to lead you to the real threat in Ustus system,"

Ares swung his battle-axes. Shattering the alien. The ice melted around them.

Sadle looked furious and outraged but Georgia just waved her silent.

"What was that about?" Georgia asked.

Ares shrugged. "Clearly the alien was deluded but remember only we know what the alien told us. And he told us about a real threat in the Ustus system,"

Georgia nodded. That was their best play.

So Georgia just smiled and nodded and didn't speak as Ares gave Sadle a watered-down version of what the deluded alien told them and Sadle agreed with Ares about travelling to the Ustus system.

Then Georgia forced herself not to laugh as Ares started spinning a wild story about the extreme danger of the Ustus system and how they were going to need every single Angel there for the assault.

Including all three loyal legions to the Emperor.

And Georgia was completely amazed when Sadle agreed to summon them to the system.

And Georgia was really, really excited about having all their superhuman and normal human enemies in one single system making it so much easier to kill them all.

CHAPTER 11

The wonderful thing about Ares's lying to Sadle was that she was now a lot more concerned about a real threat to the Empire compared to some little trial about his treachery that would be revealed soon enough, so thankfully Ares had managed to summon Luna, Legion Lord of the Sirens of the Emperor, and Georgia to his private chambers for a very secretive rebel meeting.

Ares sat on the futilely thin blue sheets of his grey superhuman bed in his box-room living quarters that he rarely used because of Angels rarely needed sleep. Ares had never really liked the bright blue walls, broken lights in the ceiling and the broken black sofa that Luna and Georgia currently sat on. Nothing in Ares's bedroom was really him anymore, so that was probably why he didn't spend much time here.

"We need a new plan," Luna said.

Ares nodded, and he was glad that Luna was here in her bright blue Angel armour that looked like such a stunning contrast to the thinner dark green uniform that Georgia had decided to wear.

"We'll arrive in the Ustus System in two months," Ares said. "By that time we need to have a perfect plan for getting rid of loyalist forces in our own ranks, we need to position ourselves to annihilate the loyalist Angels and Empire Army warships when the time is right and then we need a plan for attacking Earth,"

Luna smiled and gestured that she really wanted a drink about now.

Georgia rolled her eyes.

"What?" Ares asked.

"Ares," Georgia said. "Attacking Earth is in the far future. Right now we simply need to strip our ranks of loyalists, reveal ourselves and try to get as much power as possible before the Empire figures out what we're doing,"

"But they already have," Luna said.

Ares really hated that she was right, they had already had four Legion Lords arrested and millions of superhumans were currently being put into states of sleep for transportation back to Earth.

Ares hadn't seen any warships from the arrested Legions in days since their arrest.

Luna got up and went over to Ares's bed, lifted up the sheets and grabbed a whiskey bottle that Ares had forgotten he had stashed their years ago.

Luna ripped off the cap and took a massive slurp of it.

"We need to strip our ranks sooner rather than later," Georgia said. "I suggest each reveal the rebellion to our most trusted 100 troopers and let them be our executioners,"

Ares gave Luna a sideways look and even she didn't look that impressed, but that was probably more because there would be so few loyalists in her legion. Especially as Luna had already indoctrinated her forces into the belief that Ares was their god and must obey him.

"I doubt the loyalists in the other legions would be too happy with being arrested so that has probably helped us," Georgia said.

Ares nodded but that was probably the only benefit of what was going on.

At this point it was basically Ares's legion and the Sirens of the Emperor against three very loyal legions. Ares didn't like those odds at all.

Luna took another massive gulp of whiskey and offered the bottle to Georgia but she declined.

"What about killing Sadle?" Georgia asked.

Ares shook his head. Now he was going to have to take command of the situation.

"That cannot happen. If the Ignis legion contact her and cannot reach her they will know something is up and whatever plans we have will fail,"

"We choke the loyalists to death," Luna said.

Ares was rather surprised at that comment but he liked it.

"You want to use bioweapons?" Ares asked.

Luna nodded. "The Sirens of the Emperor have tons of them because a large rebellion and alien corruption campaign we fought a few thousand years ago,"

Ares really liked that idea. It was perfect in a way, send down everyone that he expected of being loyalists and send down the three loyal legions as well and drop virus bombs on them, the virus bombs would kill them quickly.

"We would need to pick a planet with minimal underground caves and sewage systems," Georgia said.

"Good point," Ares said. The last thing he wanted was for his enemies to lock themselves in caves, sewage systems and anywhere that was air tight so the viruses would have trouble infecting and killing them.

Luna took another massive gulp of the whiskey, finishing the bottle and took out a small handheld holographic projector.

Luna bought up the ten planets in the Ustus system. Ares was hardly pleased that five of the planets were completely covered in mostly oceans, volcanic wastelands with tons of lava pouring out and toxic gases.

But then Ares realised that the other five planets were fairly toxic to because each of them only had Empire research bases on them.

So in theory if the research bases weren't attacked before Ares, Sadle and the rest of the fleets got there then it would be hard for Ares to argue that there was a deadly enemy on the planets that had to be killed.

Yet Ares still couldn't understand why that alien had insisted there was a real threat in the system when all the data and scans said there wasn't.

Why did the alien want Ares to go here of all places?

Ares didn't have a clue but he just felt like he was going to find out soon enough and that really, really worried him.

CHAPTER 12

Georgia was so annoyed at that stupid Sadle woman, all Georgia had wanted to do was contact an old military friend that was stationed near the Ustus system so he could burn the five planets with research bases on them but Sadle didn't allow her to.

This was just getting so pathetic and Sadle was really, really starting to infuriate Georgia, and she had never done well when someone infuriated her.

Thankfully Georgia and Ares were standing on the icy cold oval bridge of the Demigod watching the fiery red planets of the Ustus system get closer and closer as their immense fleet zoomed towards them, out of the immense floor-to-ceiling windows when Sadle came up and stood right next to Georgia.

It seriously took everything in Georgia's power not to attack her there and then, but Georgia just forced herself to look at the rows upon rows of red holograms in front of her.

"The Ignis', Purifiers' and Knifers' battlegrounds

will join us within the hour," Sadle said.

Georgia gasped. Sadle had just confirmed that all three loyalist Angel legions, and their Empire Army detachments, would soon be here. That meant they would be one step closer to launching an all-out attack on the foul Empire and then their rebellion could begin.

And Georgia would be one step closer towards having all the power she had ever wanted.

The ship jerked.

Ships exploded around them.

The Demigod shot back.

"Report!" Ares shouted.

Georgia just focused on the corpses pouring out of the destroyed blade-like warships as each one finished exploding and something ripped them apart.

"My lord," a man said from the command crew. "Empire Command has sent over what the research bases in Ustus are researching,"

Georgia just knew she wasn't going to like the answer.

"There is an ancient weapon on one of the planets that creates artificial gravity creating a number of different gravitational pulls within the system," he said.

Georgia just looked at Ares. "And we just flew straight in-between two different gravitational fields,"

Ares nodded.

"Calculate the best route for a fleet this size to safely enter the system," Georgia said to the command crew.

This was hardly what they needed right now, if they made one false move that they could easily end up destroying all their forces before the loyalists had even arrived, then their rebellion was basically dead in the water.

"The Star Children know space travel better than anyone," Ares said to Sadle.

She laughed. "And they are conspirators. I will not contact the ship transporting them for one of your whims,"

Georgia had to admit that was a good try of Ares, but she just knew it was impossible to reach their allies for the time being. They were well and truly alone with Sadle and her forces.

"Commander," a man from the command crew said.

Georgia looked up at the very top tier of crew members hunched over their holographic computers and a very short woman stood up.

"It cannot be done," she said. "Our fleet is too large to travel safely into the system. The research expeditions were able to because of their small size and speed of their small ships. We do not have those qualities,"

"Thank you," Georgia said.

Ares huffed next to her and Georgia was seriously not impressed but maybe there was still a way to show the weird gravity of the system to their advantage. What if they would trick the loyalists into going into the system first?

Sadle tapped her foot next to Georgia, and Georgia really knew that Sadle would see through any deception like that because she had been here when the woman told them it was impossible to go through.

That was yet another dead end.

"There is a threat in the system," Georgia said to herself before looking at the command crew. "Can you *contact* the research bases?"

Georgia really hoped the command crew were paying attention to how carefully she said that.

"Negative me lady," a man said.

Georgia forced herself not to smile, now she only had to play it up to Sadle so at least she would remain interested in breaching the Ustus system.

"All those worlds lost," Sadle said. "This is most concerning but it is out of our hands. My mandate is to transport you-"

Ares swung his battle-axes into her chest.

Sadle's blood poured out onto the floor and splashed up the massive floor-to-ceiling windows.

Georgia felt so cheated and robbed and fucked off. That was her fucking kill.

Georgia whipped out her cannon arm. Firing at all the bloody Ignis guards.

Their chests exploded. Superhuman blood painted the floor and walls and ceiling.

Georgia screamed in frustration at that stupid woman before Ares started laughing and Georgia forced herself to get back into control.

"Well done," Ares said.

Georgia didn't understand for a moment until she saw the mutilated corpses of the ten Ignis guards. She had murdered ten superhumans and it felt amazing.

The entire command crew started clapping.

"Are we doing it then?" someone asked.

Georgia just laughed as her amazing, brilliant command crew had always known about her and Ares's rebellious intentions and they all seemed firmly behind it, and Georgia just knew if she checked the communications outside of the bridge it would be impossible to do so.

Because Georgia really loved it that the command crew had probably blocked wireless communication to make sure Sadle and her ten guards couldn't tell anyone about their little attack.

"Of course," Ares said seeming a lot calmer now.

"And you all support this?" Georgia asked.

And to her utter amazement every single member of the command crew looked at her like she was the most stupidest woman in the galaxy because they were all firmly behind burning the Empire to the ground in her's and Ares's names.

"Lokien," Georgia said. "Clean up the bodies and take, um, those two with you,"

Georgia pointed to two women belonging to the command crew and they immediately went to help Lokien start the cleaning up.

"Right then my Lord Ares," Georgia said with a massive smile. "We have an Empire to burn,"

"Indeed we do dear sister. Indeed we do,"

CHAPTER 13

Ares was so pleased to finally have that stupid woman Sadle out of his superhuman hair, because she absolutely had to be the worst enemy he had ever faced because she was so horrible and annoying and just outrageous.

Ares wiped away the dark red blood from his two massive battle-axes as he stood on the oval bridge of the Demigod as his command crew contacted Luna and all ships that Ares was 100% sure were loyal to only him and not the foul Emperor, this was the time for them to start swinging the sword that would kill the Empire once and for all.

So many rebels, mutants and rebels had tried to kill the Empire before but Ares just knew that he was the only one that could actually do it.

"Lord Ares," Luna said oddly formally as she appeared as a red hologram in the middle of the bridge. "I presume now my command crew have blocked communications I can get rid of my escorts,"

Ares laughed. He had always loved how confident and firm that Luna was, and even now with the chance of them all getting arrested and killed she didn't seem scared in the slightest.

"Confirmed," Ares said.

Luna laughed and flicked her wrist and the deafening sound of gunfire screamed over the speakers on the Demigod.

Even a splash of blood poured over Luna's chest plate.

"My entire legion have confirmed their support to you my Lord of War," Luna said. "And before you ask my Legion have a lot of tricks to communicate with each other without guards knowing,"

Ares bowed his head, at this point in time he hardly cared how the Sirens of the Emperor communicated, he was just glad to have a legion of Angels on his side.

"Ares," Georgia said walking up to him and her cannon arm tapped on the floor next to her. "I have contacted my Empire Army friends. 98% of all ships have agreed to join us,"

Ares was really impressed that meant hundreds of thousands of Empire Army warships were firmly his to command and that meant millions of troopers to use against the foul Emperor.

"I transfer command of them to you," Ares said.

Georgia gave him a mocking bow, Ares seriously loved his sister-from-another-mother.

"We must deal with the 2% now," Luna said.

"Ares!" a woman from the command crew shouted.

Ares looked at the tiers of command crew workers. "What?"

"Ten thousand Ignis ships are entering the system's boundaries. They will be here in five minutes," she said.

Ares rolled his eyes.

"And Ares," the woman said, "I detect the Fiery Deliverance is with them,"

"Fuck!" Ares shouted.

Of all the fucking warships that could have turned up, that was not the one that Ares wanted in the slightest. That was the flagship of the Lord Ignis himself, the Legion Lord of Ignis had decided to turn up.

In normal situations Ares couldn't have cared less about that little detail but the Fiery Deliverance was one of the most heavily armed warships in the Empire.

Ares looked at Georgia and Luna and the command crew. "Execute any loyalists you find. If anyone refuses to renounce their oaths to the Emperor just kill them. No torturing bullshit. No prisoners of war. No nothing. Just kill them,"

Luna and Georgia bowed before walking away to deliver the new orders and Ares just smiled because his rebellion was finally happening. After close to a decade or more of plotting, scheming and gathering his strength it was all finally happening.

"My lord," a man said sounding shy from the top tier of the command crew. "I'm detecting a large Purifier detachment behind the Ignis and the Purity Flame is with them,"

Ares just laughed. This was not what he needed.

In all honesty Ares was surprised that it had been the Ignis legion to escort him back to Earth instead of the zealot Purifiers they were the true monsters of the Empire, slaughtering anyone who dared to speak against the Emperor.

They really wouldn't hesitate to kill Ares but then Ares quickly realised that he had been played for an absolute fool.

The Dawned One or whatever alien race that alien with the leaf-shaped ship was from was Pro-Empire, and he had led Ares to a dangerous deadly system that was impossible to pass into and come to think of it Ares couldn't understand how the loyalists had gotten here so quickly.

Given the distance between their homeworld, Earth and Ares's fleet location and the Ustus system. Ares should have had to wait a week for the loyalists to turn up.

So the loyalists had to be travelling for a long time before Ares had ever started to come here.

Ares just couldn't believe how the Empire had staged everything, he didn't know how yet but he could. And Ares didn't know how the Empire had bargained with an alien for his help (if he was ever real at all) but Ares knew one thing for sure.

The Empire knew about the rebellion and they were always going to kill him.

"Ares," Georgia said. "Lord Ignis wants to speak to Sadle now,"

Ares just laughed because he was well and truly fucked. He couldn't lead the fleet into the Ustus system because it would rip the fleet apart and he couldn't escape the other way because that's where the loyalists were coming from.

Ares was going to have to do the unthinkable.

"Go up," Ares said.

"But that would leave our weaker hull armour exposed," Georgia said.

Damn it. Ares couldn't do that not with the Fiery Deliverance and the Purity Flame so close with their immense guns.

"What about below?" Ares asked.

Georgia shrugged. "Negative. I tried it once and our cannons cannot rise high enough to accurately attack the enemy from below,"

"But the enemy cannot fire on us. They don't have guns on their hull," Ares said.

"They do. And the Fiery Deliverance has twenty annihilator cannons on its hull," Georgia said.

Ares just cursed under his breath. This wasn't good and even if they travelled below the enemy they would struggle to target and damage the cannons before the Fiery Deliverance could fire on them.

They were stuck. Trapped. Dead in the water.

And Ares had absolutely no hope of escaping.

CHAPTER 14

Georgia felt absolutely amazing as she stared at the immense Ignis and Purifier fleets bearing down towards them in the cold darkness of space as she studied the enemy through the massive floor-to-ceiling windows on the oval bridge of the Demigod.

"We need a plan Ares," Georgia said.

As much as Georgia just wanted to order her Empire Army forces to attack, slaughter and annihilate the enemy, she wasn't going to do anything without the Angels under Ares's command doing something too.

She just wanted Ares to respond.

"Put the Lord Ignis through," Ares said. "And tell me immediately when the loyalists within our ranks have been slaughtered,"

Georgia nodded and just for comfort more than anything else she made sure her cannon arm was fully operational and prepared to fire. She still didn't trust Lokien who was now standing very close behind her.

Moments later a red hologram appeared in front of Ares of a very tall man in thick Angel battle armour and instead of hands he had two immense flamethrowers attached to them.

"Where is Commander Sadle?" the Lord Ignis asked.

Georgia flicked her wrists and bought up a small row of holograms that had the percentage of their forces cleared for loyalists. It was already at 50% which was rather impressive considering the sheer size of the fleet.

And Georgia was even more impressed that it seemed more and more loyal-to-Ares soldiers were joining the executioners with each passing second so hopefully the killing of the loyalists wouldn't take as long as Georgia feared.

"She is being dealt with," Ares said.

Georgia swiped the row of holograms in front of her and double-checked how much longer until the Ignis fleet were within firing range.

Thirty seconds.

Georgia went over to the closest tier of command crew workers hunched over their holographic computers.

"Order the fleet to move as close as they can to the Ustus System without getting ripped apart and see if you can plot us a course through the different gravitational pulls," Georgia said.

All the command crew members within earshot gave her a weary smile.

"Sadle is dead," Ares said.

Georgia had not been expecting Ares to reveal that so soon. The fleet was still only 62% cleared of loyalists. They needed more time.

"That is most regrettable to hear," Lord Ignis said. "Out of the sake of our shared history and the respect I once held for you-"

Ares waved him silent. "I am not surrendering. All forces battle stations!"

Georgia cut the line with Lord Ignis and just looked at Ares.

"Battle stations?" Georgia asked.

Ares shrugged. "We've been forced into a corner. Contact your forces tell them to give no quarter,"

Georgia nodded as she relayed the new orders to her Empire Army forces and she flicked her wrists and the red hologram changed to reveal the battle.

The Demigod shook.

Georgia felt the Demigod open fire.

Cannons roared.

Guns fired.

Lasers flew through space.

Smashing into the enemy.

Georgia's ships shattered. Smashed. Exploded.

The Ignis were zooming towards them.

They were trapped. Georgia didn't have an escape route.

The Fiery Deliverance was almost within range.

Someone tackled Georgia to the ground.

Superhuman hands wrapped round her throat.

The bridge door exploded open.

Superhuman bullets screamed through the air. Loyalists were attacking.

Georgia smashed her fists into her attacker.

He fell off her.

Georgia jumped up.

Georgia saw Lokien whip out his gun.

Georgia whipped up her cannon arm. She fired.

The cannon blasted off him.

Lokien fired.

Georgia dived to one side.

Ares screamed in rage.

Loyalist Angels flooded the bridge. They fired at the command crew. The crew were dying.

The Demigod jerked.

Ships around it were dying.

They were losing forces.

Warships were burning. The loyalists were winning.

Lokien shot Georgia in the leg. Her leg shattered. She screamed.

Lokien ran at her. Punching her in the chest.

Ribs broke. Georgia gasped for air. She couldn't breathe.

Lokien whipped out a knife. He swung at her.

Georgia forced herself to breathe. She barely managed.

Georgia ducked.

Catching Lokien off balance. He fell to the ground.

Georgia smashed her cannon into his head. She fired.

Lokien's head exploded.

Red flashing warning lights screamed overhead. The Demigod was losing systems.

The loyalist Angels kept firing.

Ares flew forward. Swinging his battle-axes. Chomping into their flesh.

Georgia kept firing.

Traitor Angels swarmed in behind the loyalists. Slaughtering them.

Within moments the entire bridge was clear of all loyalist Angels and the few baseline humans that had dared to join them but half of the command crew were dead.

The Demigod couldn't function without a command crew.

The Demigod vibrated. Something exploded.

Georgia collapsed to the ground as immense pain flooded her body from the shattered leg.

The Demigod screamed in protest as cannons slammed into it. Its shields failed. Fire engulfed more sections.

The Demigod was dying.

Ares rushed over to Georgia. He quickly took off his hand's armour and sliced his hand. Smearing the superhuman blood on the wound.

Georgia just hoped Ares's superhuman biology could help her.

Alarms screamed overhead as Georgia knew that

the Demigod's anti-missile system activated.

Georgia just knew the Fiery Deliverance had launched their most powerful weapon at them. The Demigod couldn't survive that.

Georgia checked the percentage of the fleet cleared. It was done. No more loyalists existed in their forces.

"It's done," Georgia told Ares.

A warship zoomed above the Demigod. The missile smashed into it. Shattering it.

The shockwave threw Georgia across the bridge. Ares suffered the same.

So much of their forces were destroyed. They couldn't survive this. This had always been a stupid plan.

"My Lord!" someone shouted.

Georgia hissed in pain as she felt the superhuman blood heal her wounds.

"Reinforcements have arrived!" a woman said.

Georgia couldn't have cared less about Empire reinforcements at this point.

"What? Knifer Legion?" Ares asked.

"No!" a man shouted. "The five arrested legions. They're here. Requesting your orders,"

Georgia forced herself up. This was the time to fucking annihilate these loyalist scum that had destroyed so many of her forces.

"Burn them all!" Ares shouted.

CHAPTER 15

Ares seriously didn't care how the amazing traitor legions had escaped their Ignis escorts, he was just flat out amazed at them and how willing they were to help. Clearly they were just as pissed off with the Empire as he was. Something as he stood on the oval bridge of the Demigod he was going to make sure paid in their favour.

"Burn them all!" Ares shouted.

The entire Demigod shook violently as every single weapon fired on the blade-like flagship. Ares watched the cannons and bullets and other weapons smash into the foul Empire.

Ignis warships exploded, shattered and burned.

The Fiery Deliverance fired.

Warships exploded around Ares.

The Ignis surged forward. Their fleet would swarm them within moments.

He needed a plan.

The four arrested Legions were slaughtering the

Purifiers. They were too far away from Ares to help him for now.

More warships shattered around Ares.

Ares watched the warning lights. He couldn't run away from this fight. He wanted to burn the Empire.

He really needed to destroy the Fiery Deliverance as a statement of his rebellion. He needed to shatter these legions.

Ares flicked his wrists. The red hologram zoomed in showing the Ignis fleet. It was massive.

But there was a critical weakness. It was in a very standard formation that had a single weakness.

If Ares swarmed the Ignis instead of the other way around the Ignis would be too surprised to counteract his attack.

Ares had no clue if his forces would survive it. They were beaten, weakened and barely alive.

All Ares needed to do was get to the 4 arrested legions and flee with them then he would be fine. He knew Luna was waiting for Ares to make a move.

Massive explosions lit up the void.

The Star Children were slaughtering the Purifiers. It still didn't help Ares.

Ares was just going to have to do it. No matter the risk.

He relayed the orders to the surviving command crew. They didn't even question the order.

Even Georgia was oddly silent as she relayed the orders to her forces.

The Demigod zoomed forward.

The Ignis fleet got larger and larger as Ares got closer and closer.

The Demigod shook violently.

The Ignis were firing on them.

The Fiery Deliverance was preparing to fire.

Ares ordered the entire fleet to throw everything they had at the Fiery Deliverance once they were within range.

Ares's fleet surged forward. Getting closer to the target.

More ships exploded. More ships died. Hundreds of crews were massacred.

Ares made the fleet hold course.

The Demigod shook. More fires erupted all over the ship. More requests for aid filled the bridge.

The Fiery Deliverance was so close. Ares could see it.

"Fire!" Ares shouted.

The Fiery Deliverance fired too.

The Demigod flew to one side to avoid the attack.

It failed.

The Demigod's engines exploded. Decks of the ship turned to ash.

The engines exploded.

The weapons systems shattered.

Screaming alarms echoed around the bridge.

Ares just hoped the bridge would survive.

The Fiery Deliverance lit up the void as it exploded and millions of loyalist Angels died too.

"Evacuate the ship," Georgia said.

Ares watched the Ignis fleet behind them start to retreat and forget about Ares's forces as they zoomed towards the Ustus system only to be ripped apart by the gravitational forces.

Ares was just glad the Demigod was being left alone by the enemy as it was basically a sitting duck and Ares just knew it was only a matter of time before the ship exploded.

But as the Demigod shifted towards the surviving Sirens of the Emperor ships and saw them preparing to extract Ares and Georgia and any other survivors from the Demigod, he just knew that the rebellion would survive.

And because the four other legions had been arrested and attacked by the Empire for breaking a simple law. There would be a hell of a hunger for revenge and hatred against the Empire.

So Ares just smiled because now his rebellion could escape into the depths of space, gather their forces and well and truly start to burn the Empire to the ground.

Just as he always wanted.

CHAPTER 16

Georgia sat on a wonderfully cool metal chair in a very large meeting chamber on the flagship of the Hydra Legion, that was strangely called *The Hydra's Truth*, which was an odd name for a legion that dedicated itself to spy work, disinformation and spreading as many lies as they possibly could.

Georgia rather liked the smooth bright red walls of the meeting chamber that was square-shaped with a few pieces of holographic art on the walls, giving the meeting chamber a sense of peace and calm and stability in a situation that was far from it.

The meeting chamber smelt warming of cinnamon, cloves and soaked fruits that reminded Georgia of "Christmas" myths that her grandmother read from a history book as they debated the meaning of the legends from Ancient earth. Even though Georgia knew the rest of the ship and fleet and beyond was a hive of activity as everyone prepared for the Empire to attack them again, Georgia was really pleased that the meeting chamber was rather silent with only the odd tapping of footsteps above them and the ship's humming and vibrating breaking the silence from time to time.

Even the large bright red oval table in front of Georgia was a nice touch that she doubted the Hydra legion were actually capable of, it was certainly a focal point for the meeting chamber, but in a nasty or aggressive sense like so much that the Hydra Legion did.

In fact Georgia wouldn't have been surprised if this was one of the few chambers on any of the Hydra Legion's ships that was actually an honest reflection of what the legion were (at least one point in time), and that was a legion dedicated to peace and stability and actually sitting down with their friends and talking out their problems.

Something that Georgia was hoping the Hydra legion would be willing to do now, especially as the other traitor legions were helping Ares's and Luna's legion sort out what was damaged, what needed replacing and anything else that they needed after the battle.

Georgia rested her massive cannon arm on the table and she knew whatever the Hydra Legion wanted in their little war that would decide their position in the rebellion, they would easily get it. Because Georgia wasn't in the arguing mood and after the battle with the Empire she definitely needed to stabilise the rebellion and re-ascertain herself and

Ares as the leaders.

A few moments later Ares wearing his thick black armour and two massive battle-axes on his back walked in smiling, and the Hydra in his blood red battle armour came in behind him, both Legion Lords sat down close to Georgia and all three of them smiled.

And Georgia quickly realised that the power dynamic of the rebellion hadn't shifted as much as she feared. She had always been concerned that the other traitor legions wouldn't see Ares as strong anymore because they had saved him, but Georgia had clearly forgotten the impact of destroying the Fiery Deliverance.

The defacto flagship of the Empire.

"What is the power structure?" the Hydra asked.

Out of all the conversations about where to strike, where to destroy and what installations across the Empire Georgia and Ares needed to annihilate, the actual power structure within the rebellion had never really come up. In fact they had sort of always assumed that Ares would be in charge of the Angels and Georgia would be in charge of all non-Angel assets.

Which might not have sounded too exciting to people outside of Georgia's and Ares's sibling-ly bond but Georgia just knew that was a hell of a lot of trust for an Angel to trust a mere baseline human with.

"Your question is wrong," Ares said. "You want a position in the ranks of my inner circle and you will have it Hydra,"

Georgia just laughed as the Hydra's superhuman face twisted in complete surprise.

"There will be no bargaining, no tricks, no nothing," Georgia said. "I think I am right in saying we want you to lead our spy network,"

Ares nodded and Georgia was relieved they were on the same page.

"That is correct," Ares said. "Your duty to us is to infiltrate Empire worlds, Legions and Empire Army units. We need as much intelligence as possible about the Empire and most importantly how to destroy them,"

The Hydra seemed genuinely pleased with the outcome, and now Georgia was slightly curious as to why the Hydra doubted he would ever be in a top position. The Hydra was an amazing spymaster and maybe the best in the galaxy, if that didn't qualify him for a top job then Georgia wasn't sure what did.

"Thank you my Lords," the Hydra said. "And as a gesture of good faith I will have my Legion transmit all reports to both of you my Lords,"

Georgia was even more surprised when the Hydra bowed at both of them and actually gestured that he wanted to kiss Georgia's hand, and she let him.

As the Hydra left, Georgia was flat out stunned that she had managed to win over such a harsh critic of her as a mere baseline human that didn't have the strength, power or biology of an Angel.

"What won him over?" Georgia asked.

Ares laughed. "The simple fact that all the traitor legions know the Empire has disowned them. They need our protection a lot more than we need theirs for now,"

Georgia smiled because there was something very powering and intoxicating about that all alone.

"You know Ares," Georgia said, "I've always wondered how the traitor legions escaped?"

Ares nodded. "Good question. The Hydra and the other Legion Lords along with some troopers all tell the same consistent story and it is that the Raven Crow legion had already heavily infiltrated the Ignis legion,"

Georgia smiled because she really knew this was going to get good.

"So when the captured Angels and Legion Lords were being escorted back to Earth, our spies on the ships took the initiative and started to sabotage the sleep-chambers the Angels were kept in. Forcing them to awaken and then the Raven Crow armed them, and over the course of a few hours each ship was taken over and they raced towards Ustus,"

Georgia was so pleased to have the Raven Crow and Hydra legion in charge, at least that meant that the Empire no longer had superhumans that specialised in infiltration and spy work.

But Georgia also knew that the sad truth was the Empire still had a lot more resources, baseline human spies and other assets at their disposal, yet that was tomorrow's problem.

As Georgia and Ares started planning, plotting and scheming some more about their next moves, Georgia was filled with such a sense of pride and amazement that after so long she finally had everything she had ever wanted in life.

She had an amazing best friend and brother-from-another-mother in Ares, she had all the power she had ever wanted and finally Georgia was going to make sure she got the respect from the Empire that she had always deserved but never received.

And that was a truly amazing feeling to have and one that Georgia was going to treasure for a long, long time.

CHAPTER 17

As Ares stood in his brand-new massive lab with its bright white walls, orbs of light above him and single metal slab in the centre of the lab, Ares was so excited to the amazing future and he really loved watching all of his medical instruments swirl, twirled and work away on the tall chunk of flesh he was currently working on as the instruments hung down from the ceiling.

Ares actually preferred this lab on his new flagship that Luna had gifted him as a present, along with a much more serious token of her legion's loyalty to him by changing their name from Sirens of the Emperor to the Sirens of War.

Ares was still truly honoured because Luna was surprisingly enough one of his closest friends now, and Ares could really see himself relying on her in the decades to come, because when he first met her he really didn't like her, but Luna was smart, cunning and an amazing friend.

And she knew exactly how to use religion and people's faith in Ares as a living god to manipulate and control them. That was something Ares loved about Luna.

She really was amazing.

The only problem with the new lab was that it still had the faint smell of the foul burning incense that the Sirens of War seemed to be obsessed with burning at every chance they got, so Ares was definitely going to upgrade the ship's cleaning systems so the smell would be a thing of the past.

The instruments operating on the fleshy chunk on the metal slab hummed a little more and Ares was really excited.

Ares seriously hoped that his experiment this time would work and that he would finally be able to create a robotic human that looked identical to the real thing.

If this worked then it would change the course of the war, and Ares could finally have his own spy network that reported only to him and Georgia and he wouldn't have to rely so much on the dam Hydra legion that Ares still wasn't too sure on.

The sound of the ship humming, vibrating and popping echoed around the lab as Ares knew that his forces were preparing to travel to their first target of the rebellion, the small agri-system of Hemicus so that would destroy the food supply routes for the Empire Army and that was a perfect target to start off with.

And that was only the beginning.

"Commander Georgia is here to see you," a computerised voice said.

Ares flicked his wrists and the large round metal door opened and Georgia walked in, with her large cannon arm freshly painted black and it really suited her. Ares probably should have got his battle-axes painted but that was tomorrow's problem.

"Everything is ready to go," Georgia said.

Ares smiled that was great news and soon the Empire would certainly learn that the rebellion was far, far from dead.

"Thank you," Ares said. "But I have to admit the Empire was clever to set us up,"

Georgia shrugged. "I suppose so but you never told me how they did it and how did they learn about the rebellion in the first place,"

"I suspect the Hydra legion told them," Ares said.

Georgia gasped but nodded like she understood, and Ares couldn't blame her. It would seem so silly for the Hydra legion to "accidentally" tell the Empire about a rebellion they were a part of, but in reality it made perfect sense.

It was probably the biggest double cross he had ever seen, the Hydra Legion pretended to work with the Empire on a plan to capture, arrest and if it came to it destroy Ares.

The Empire probably offered the Hydra and his legion full immunity if the Hydra legion helped the

Empire to make sure Ares was in a certain location at a particular time and he didn't reveal the rebellion before he was arrested, then the Hydra probably had a hand in the arrests and making sure the other Legion Lords broke the rules so they and their legions were arrested.

It was so clever.

And maybe the biggest piece of circumstantial evidence for the Hydra's involvement was, how did the arrested legions know Ares's and Luna's and Georgia's forces were heading for the Ustus system.

It was possible the loyalists told them but it was much more likely the loyalists and other Ignis forces had wiped that information from their ships when the Raven Crow started to take over the ship.

So the Hydra legion had to know before all of this went down.

Then Ares was hardly surprised when the Empire probably recruited some desperate alien for a mission to lure Ares into believing he was safe and secure and he was going to win, and whilst Ares just knew the Hydra legion weren't behind the Empire sending the false intel about the destroyed Noir system to them specifically, Ares would have been surprised if they didn't at least have a small hand in the matter.

So Ares told Georgia all of this.

"But the alien was still right in a way," Georgia said.

Ares didn't understand what she meant.

"We could never understand why the alien or

Dawned One wanted us to travel to the Ustus system for a "real threat" that never existed,"

Ares nodded, that was definitely something that had been annoying the life out of him.

"But we know the alien attacked the Noir System to give some evidence to the false intelligence we received so it would lure us to the Noir System, which would eventually lead us to the Ustus system where I bet the Empire wanted us to be ripped apart in the different gravitational pulls."

Ares nodded at least she was making sense.

"Yet the real threat was what we became at the Ustus system," Georgia said. "The Dawned One spoke of timestreams, being Pro-Empire and more nonsense that I care to forget. To the Dawned One, us revealing the rebellion was the greatest threat to the Empire had ever existed,"

"So by the Empire recruiting an alien that spirited us along a timestream where we revealed our rebellion and started a galactic civil war, the Empire doomed themselves and their plan backfired?" Ares asked.

Georgia nodded. "If you believe in timelines and all that techy stuff then yes. The Empire has already started to kill itself and now we just need to finish the job,"

Ares laughed because it didn't sound confusing in the slightest and it was just so typical of the stupid Empire to doom themselves instead of saving themselves.

And when Ares became Emperor, he was definitely never going to fall into that trap, and he certainly wasn't going to make that mistake during the rebellion's war to control the Empire.

A massive woosh filled the lab as the instruments working on the fleshy chunk on the metal slab in the middle of the lab finished their work and rose up into the ceiling.

Ares and Georgia both carefully went over to the metal slab and Georgia just gasped, and Ares's mouth simply dropped as both of them stared at a very beautiful and perfectly created robot that looked identical to a real-life flesh and blood human.

Ares had done it, and now he could finally use them as his own private agents throughout the entire Great Human Empire, and it suddenly hit Ares that his rebellion was well and truly underway.

And despite all the problems he was going to face, Ares was seriously looking forward to dealing with them tomorrow and well and truly burning the Empire to the ground.

But today Ares just looked at Georgia and hugged her. She was his best friend and sister and no matter what happened in the decades to come, he was going to protect this beautiful woman no matter what.

Because as the feelings of happiness, delight and power flooded him, and made him feel the best he ever had, Ares just knew that family was the most important thing when facing an impossible foe.

So much so there wasn't a single other person

Ares would rather have at his side as he burned the galaxy to the ground.

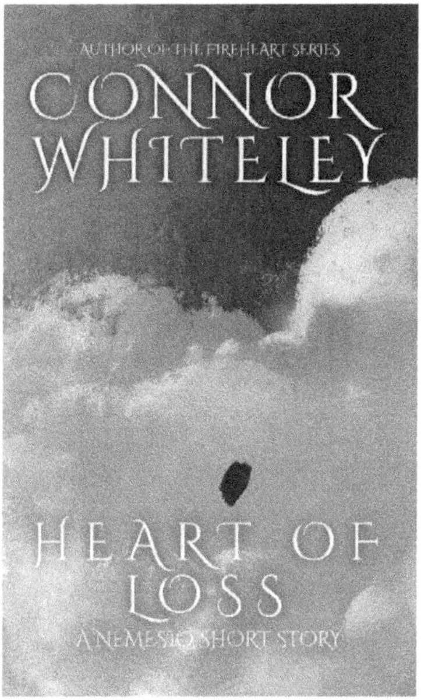

GET YOUR FREE AND EXCLUSIVE SHORT STORY NOW! LEARN ABOUT NEMESIO'S PAST!

https://www.subscribepage.com/fireheart

Keep up to date with exclusive deals on Connor Whiteley's Books, as well as the latest news about new releases and so much more!

Sign up for the Grab a Book and Chill Monthly newsletter, and you'll get one **FREE** ebook just for signing up: Agents of The Emperor Collection.

Sign Up Now!

https://dl.bookfunnel.com/f4p5xkprbk

About the author:

Connor Whiteley is the author of over 60 books in the sci-fi fantasy, nonfiction psychology and books for writer's genre and he is a Human Branding Speaker and Consultant.

He is a passionate warhammer 40,000 reader, psychology student and author.

Who narrates his own audiobooks and he hosts The Psychology World Podcast.

All whilst studying Psychology at the University of Kent, England.

Also, he was a former Explorer Scout where he gave a speech to the Maltese President in August 2018 and he attended Prince Charles' 70th Birthday Party at Buckingham Palace in May 2018.

Plus, he is a self-confessed coffee lover!

OTHER SHORT STORIES BY CONNOR WHITELEY

Mystery Short Stories:

Protecting The Woman She Hated

Finding A Royal Friend

Our Woman In Paris

Corrupt Driving

A Prime Assassination

Jubilee Thief

Jubilee, Terror, Celebrations

Negative Jubilation

Ghostly Jubilation

Killing For Womenkind

A Snowy Death

Miracle Of Death

A Spy In Rome

The 12:30 To St Pancreas

A Country In Trouble

A Smokey Way To Go

A Spicy Way To GO

A Marketing Way To Go

A Missing Way To Go

A Showering Way To Go

Poison In The Candy Cane

Christmas Innocence

You Better Watch Out

Christmas Theft

Trouble In Christmas
Smell of The Lake
Problem In A Car
Theft, Past and Team
Embezzler In The Room
A Strange Way To Go
A Horrible Way To Go
Ann Awful Way To Go
An Old Way To Go
A Fishy Way To Go
A Pointy Way To Go
A High Way To Go
A Fiery Way To Go
A Glassy Way To Go
A Chocolatey Way To Go
Kendra Detective Mystery Collection Volume 1
Kendra Detective Mystery Collection Volume 2
Stealing A Chance At Freedom
Glassblowing and Death
Theft of Independence
Cookie Thief
Marble Thief
Book Thief
Art Thief
Mated At The Morgue

The Big Five Whoopee Moments
Stealing An Election
Mystery Short Story Collection Volume 1
Mystery Short Story Collection Volume 2
Criminal Performance
Candy Detectives
Key To Birth In The Past

Science Fiction Short Stories:
Temptation
Superhuman Autospy
Blood In The Redwater
All Is Dust
Vigil
Emperor Forgive Us
Their Brave New World
Gummy Bear Detective
The Candy Detective
What Candies Fear
The Blurred Image
Shattered Legions
The First Rememberer
Life of A Rememberer
System of Wonder
Lifesaver
Remarkable Way She Died
The Interrogation of Annabella Stormic

Blade of The Emperor
Arbiter's Truth
Computation of Battle
Old One's Wrath
Puppets and Masters
Ship of Plague
Interrogation
Edge of Failure
One Way Choice
Acceptable Losses
Balance of Power
Good Idea At The Time
Escape Plan
Escape In The Hesitation
Inspiration In Need
Singing Warriors
Knowledge is Power
Killer of Polluters
Climate of Death
The Family Mailing Affair
Defining Criminality
The Martian Affair
A Cheating Affair
The Little Café Affair
Mountain of Death
Prisoner's Fight
Claws of Death

Bitter Air
Honey Hunt
Blade On A Train
<u>Fantasy Short Stories:</u>
City of Snow
City of Light
City of Vengeance
Dragons, Goats and Kingdom
Smog The Pathetic Dragon
Don't Go In The Shed
The Tomato Saver
The Remarkable Way She Died
The Bloodied Rose
Asmodia's Wrath
Heart of A Killer
Emissary of Blood
Dragon Coins
Dragon Tea
Dragon Rider
Sacrifice of the Soul
Heart of The Flesheater
Heart of The Regent
Heart of The Standing
Feline of The Lost
Heart of The Story
City of Fire
Awaiting Death

Other books by Connor Whiteley:

Bettie English Private Eye Series

A Very Private Woman

The Russian Case

A Very Urgent Matter

A Case Most Personal

Trains, Scots and Private Eyes

The Federation Protects

Lord of War Origin Trilogy:

Not Scared Of The Dark

Madness

Burn It All

The Fireheart Fantasy Series

Heart of Fire

Heart of Lies

Heart of Prophecy

Heart of Bones

Heart of Fate

City of Assassins (Urban Fantasy)

City of Death

City of Marytrs

City of Pleasure

City of Power

<u>Agents of The Emperor</u>
Return of The Ancient Ones
Vigilance
Angels of Fire
Kingmaker
The Eight
The Lost Generation
<u>Lord Of War Trilogy (Agents of The Emperor)</u>
Not Scared Of The Dark
Madness
Burn It All Down

<u>The Garro Series- Fantasy/Sci-fi</u>
GARRO: GALAXY'S END
GARRO: RISE OF THE ORDER
GARRO: END TIMES
GARRO: SHORT STORIES
GARRO: COLLECTION
<u>GARRO: HERESY</u>
<u>GARRO: FAITHLESS</u>
<u>GARRO: DESTROYER OF WORLDS</u>
<u>GARRO: COLLECTIONS BOOK 4-6</u>
GARRO: MISTRESS OF BLOOD
GARRO: BEACON OF HOPE
GARRO: END OF DAYS

All books in 'An Introductory Series':

Careers In Psychology

Psychology of Suicide

Dementia Psychology

Forensic Psychology of Terrorism And Hostage-Taking

Forensic Psychology of False Allegations

Year In Psychology

BIOLOGICAL PSYCHOLOGY 3RD EDITION

COGNITIVE PSYCHOLOGY THIRD EDITION

SOCIAL PSYCHOLOGY- 3RD EDITION

ABNORMAL PSYCHOLOGY 3RD EDITION

PSYCHOLOGY OF RELATIONSHIPS- 3RD EDITION

DEVELOPMENTAL PSYCHOLOGY 3RD EDITION

HEALTH PSYCHOLOGY

RESEARCH IN PSYCHOLOGY

A GUIDE TO MENTAL HEALTH AND TREATMENT AROUND THE WORLD- A GLOBAL LOOK AT DEPRESSION

FORENSIC PSYCHOLOGY

THE FORENSIC PSYCHOLOGY OF THEFT, BURGLARY AND OTHER

CRIMES AGAINST PROPERTY
CRIMINAL PROFILING: A FORENSIC PSYCHOLOGY GUIDE TO FBI PROFILING AND GEOGRAPHICAL AND STATISTICAL PROFILING.
CLINICAL PSYCHOLOGY
FORMULATION IN PSYCHOTHERAPY
PERSONALITY PSYCHOLOGY AND INDIVIDUAL DIFFERENCES
CLINICAL PSYCHOLOGY REFLECTIONS VOLUME 1
CLINICAL PSYCHOLOGY REFLECTIONS VOLUME 2
Clinical Psychology Reflections Volume 3
CULT PSYCHOLOGY
Police Psychology

A Psychology Student's Guide To University
How Does University Work?
A Student's Guide To University And Learning
University Mental Health and Mindset

www.ingramcontent.com/pod-product-compliance
Lightning Source LLC
LaVergne TN
LVHW012119070526
838202LV00056B/5783
9781915551931